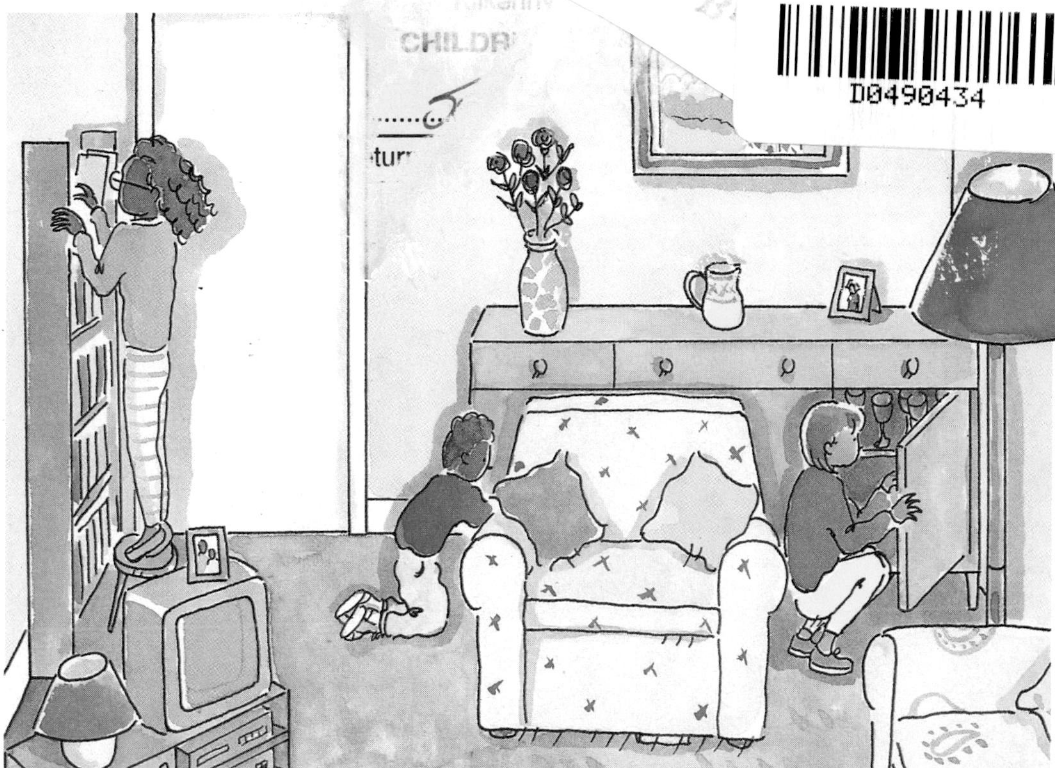

Look.

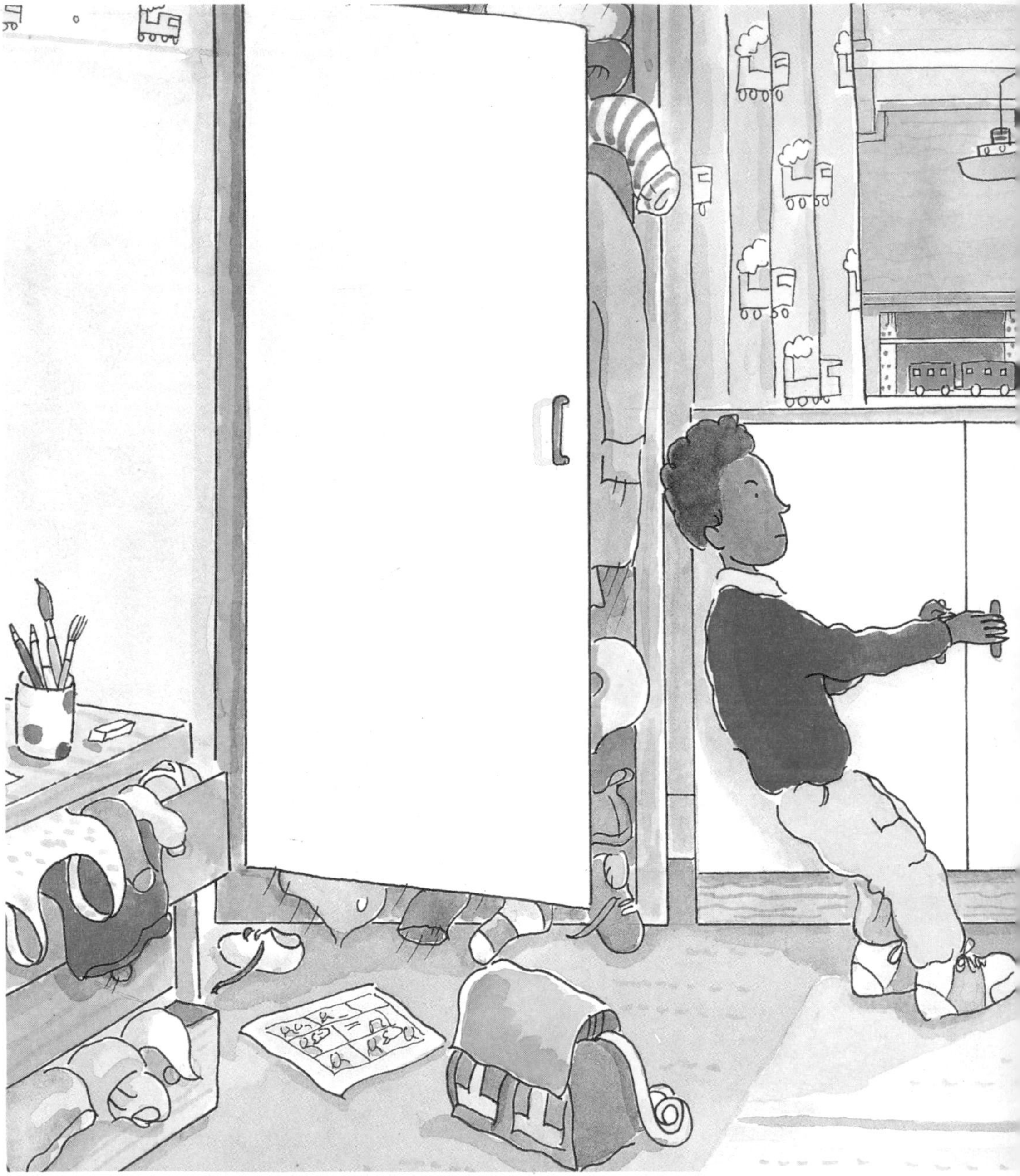

Look in here.

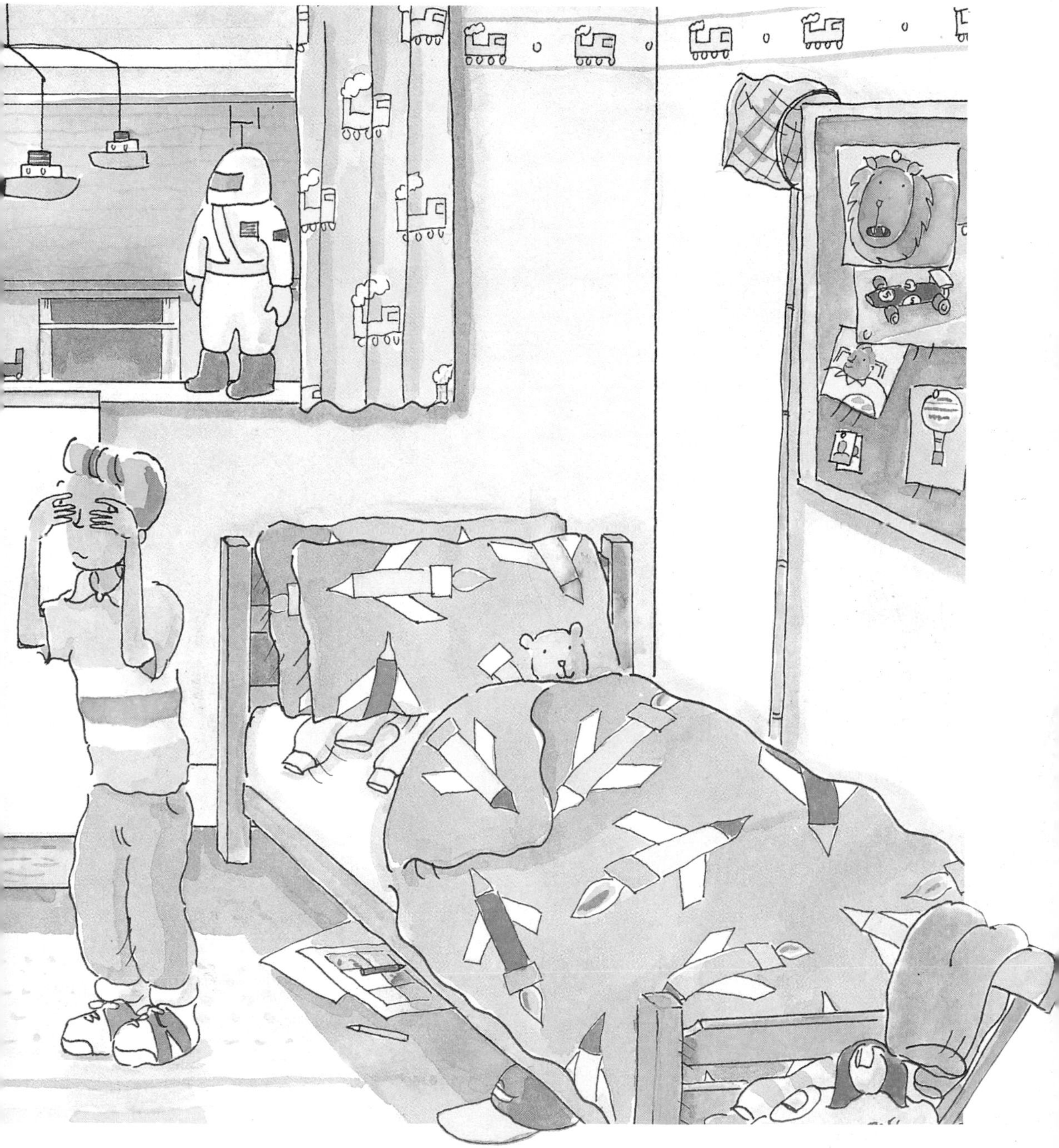

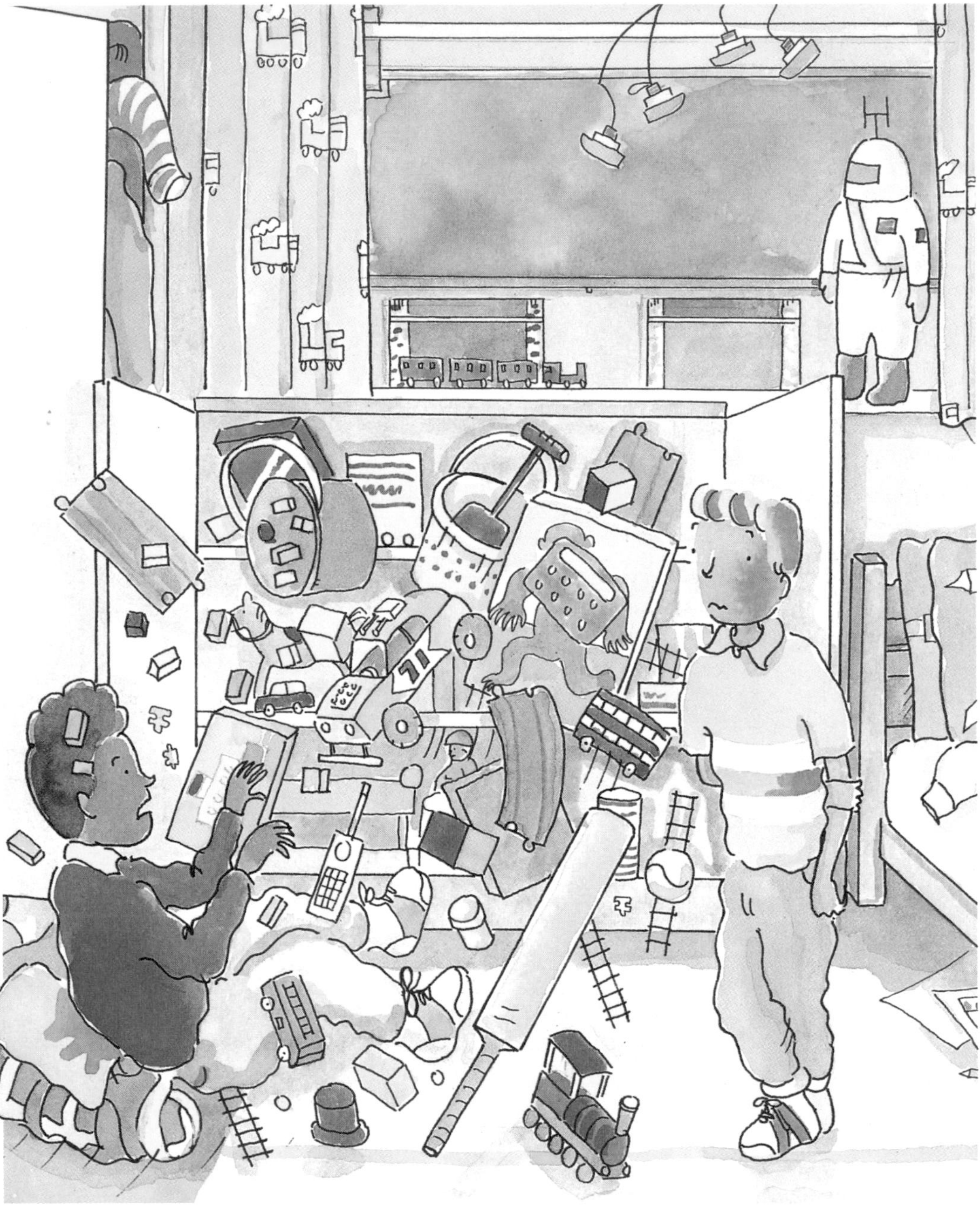

No.

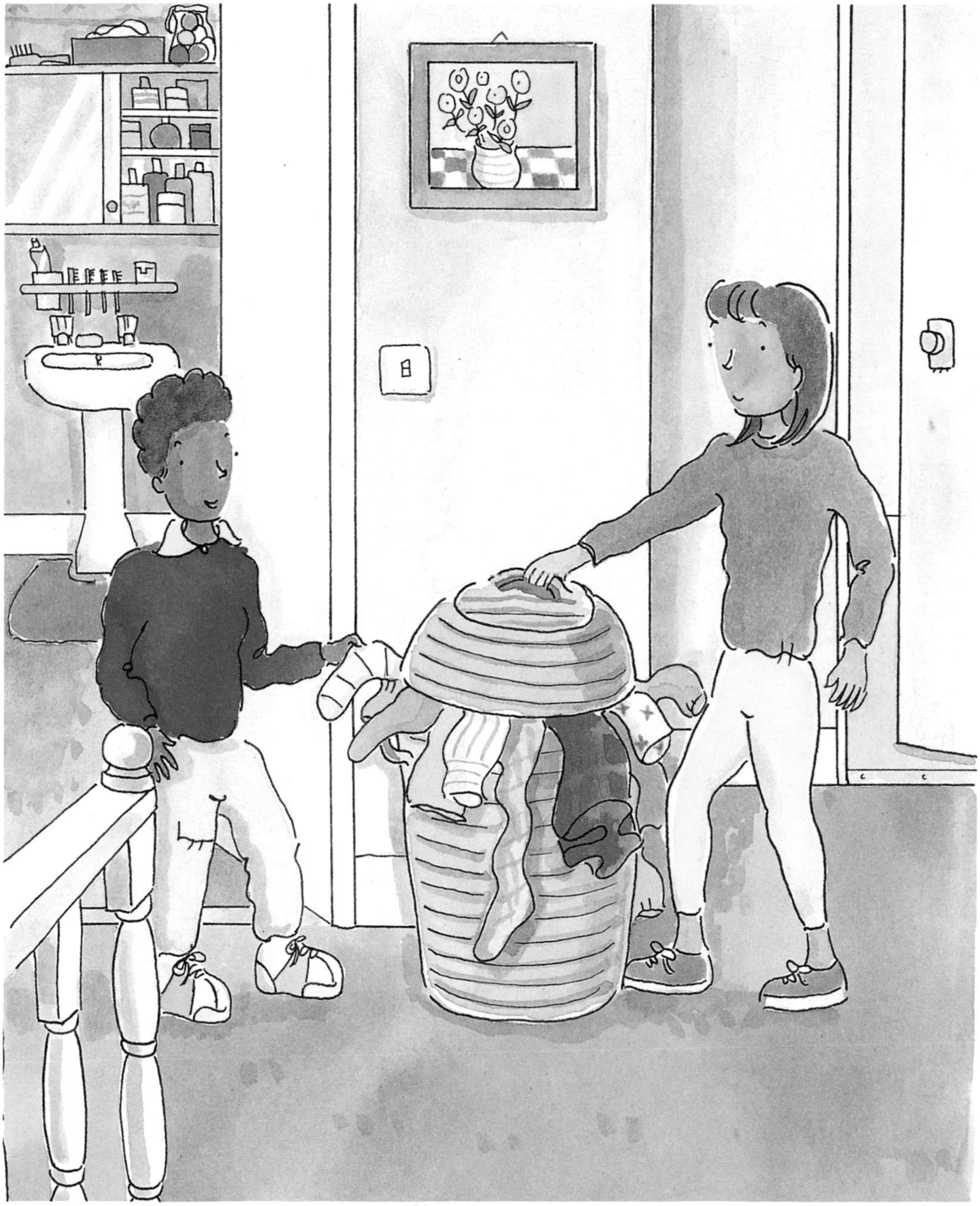

Look in here.

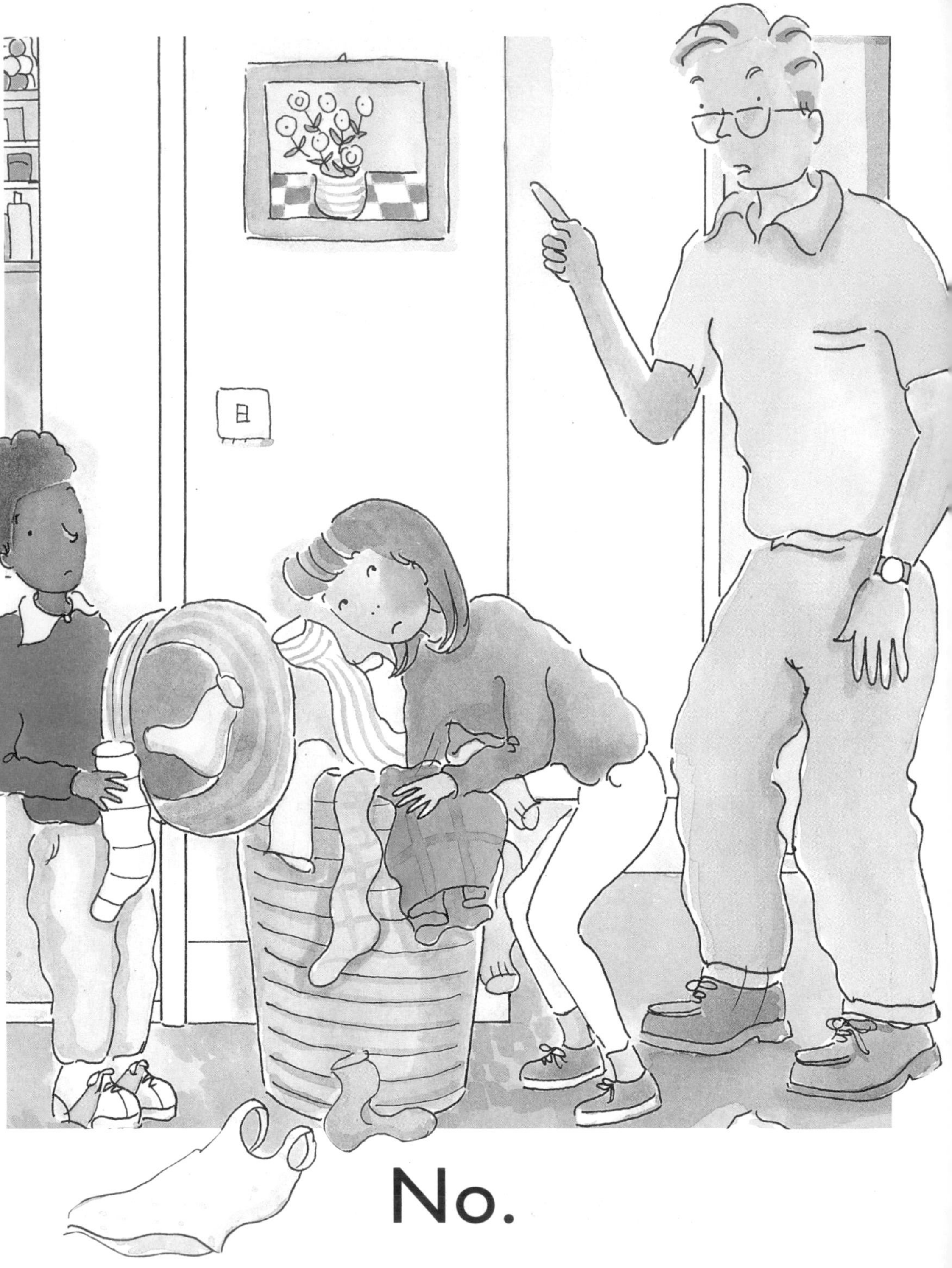

No.

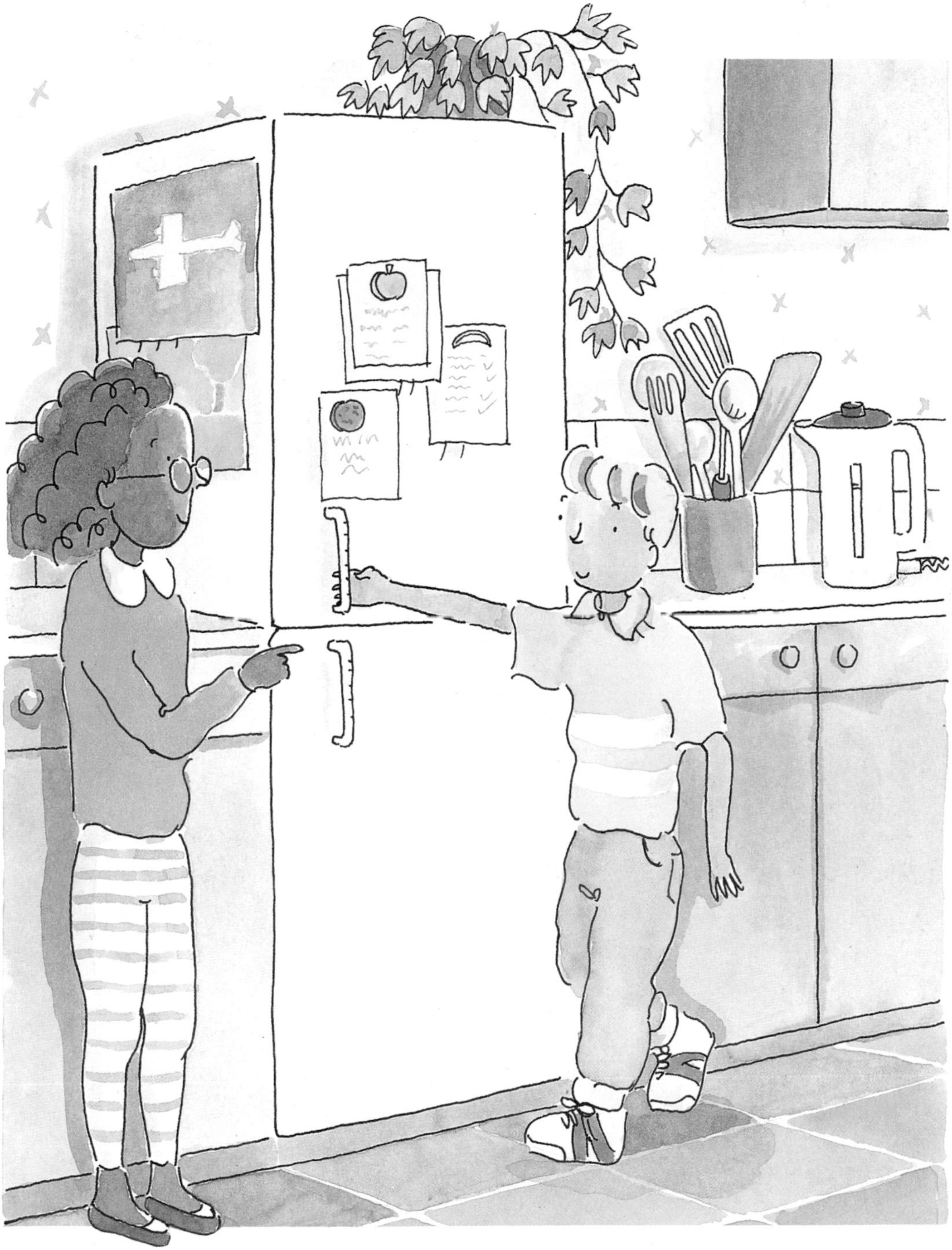

Look in here.

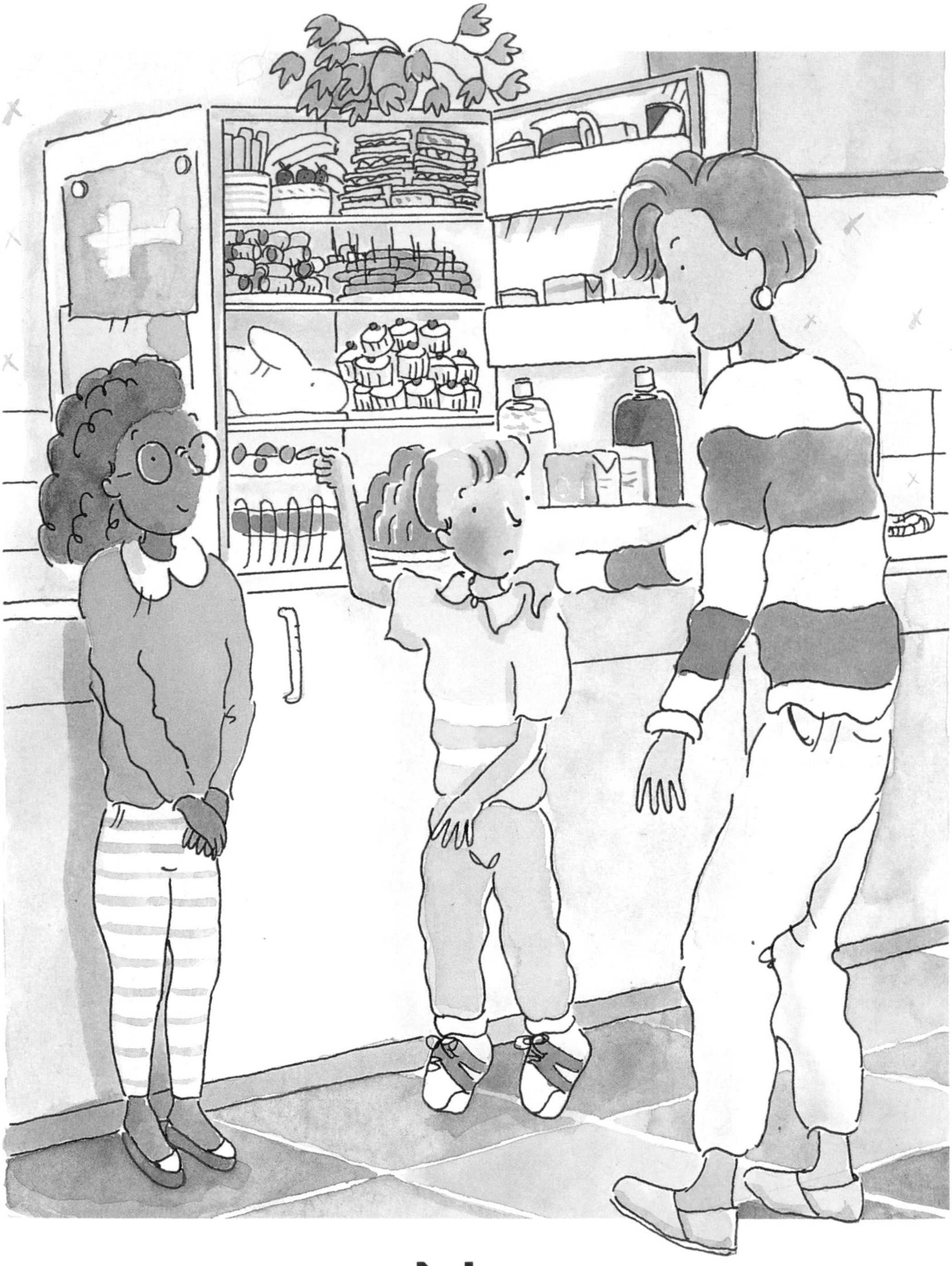

No.

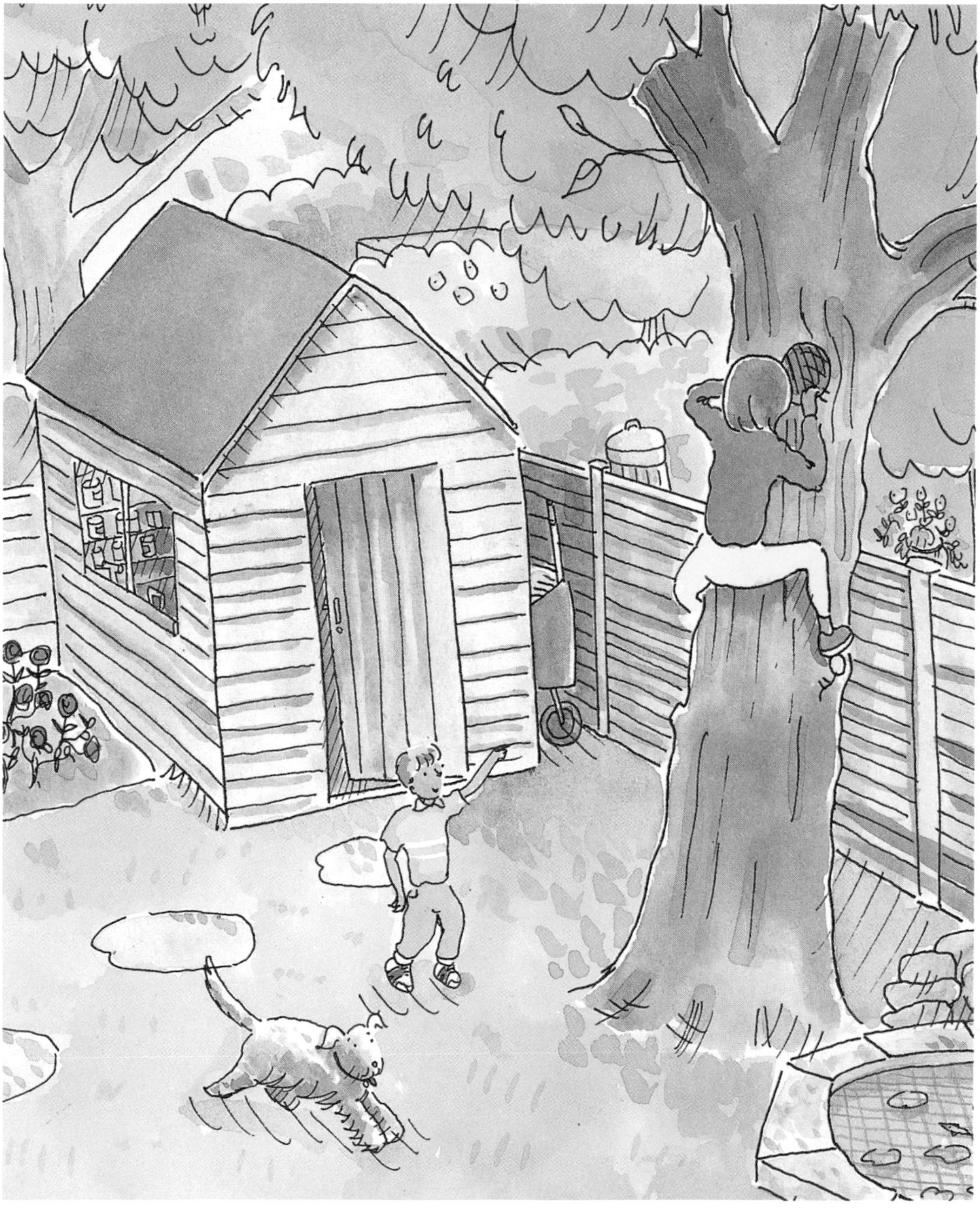

Look in here.

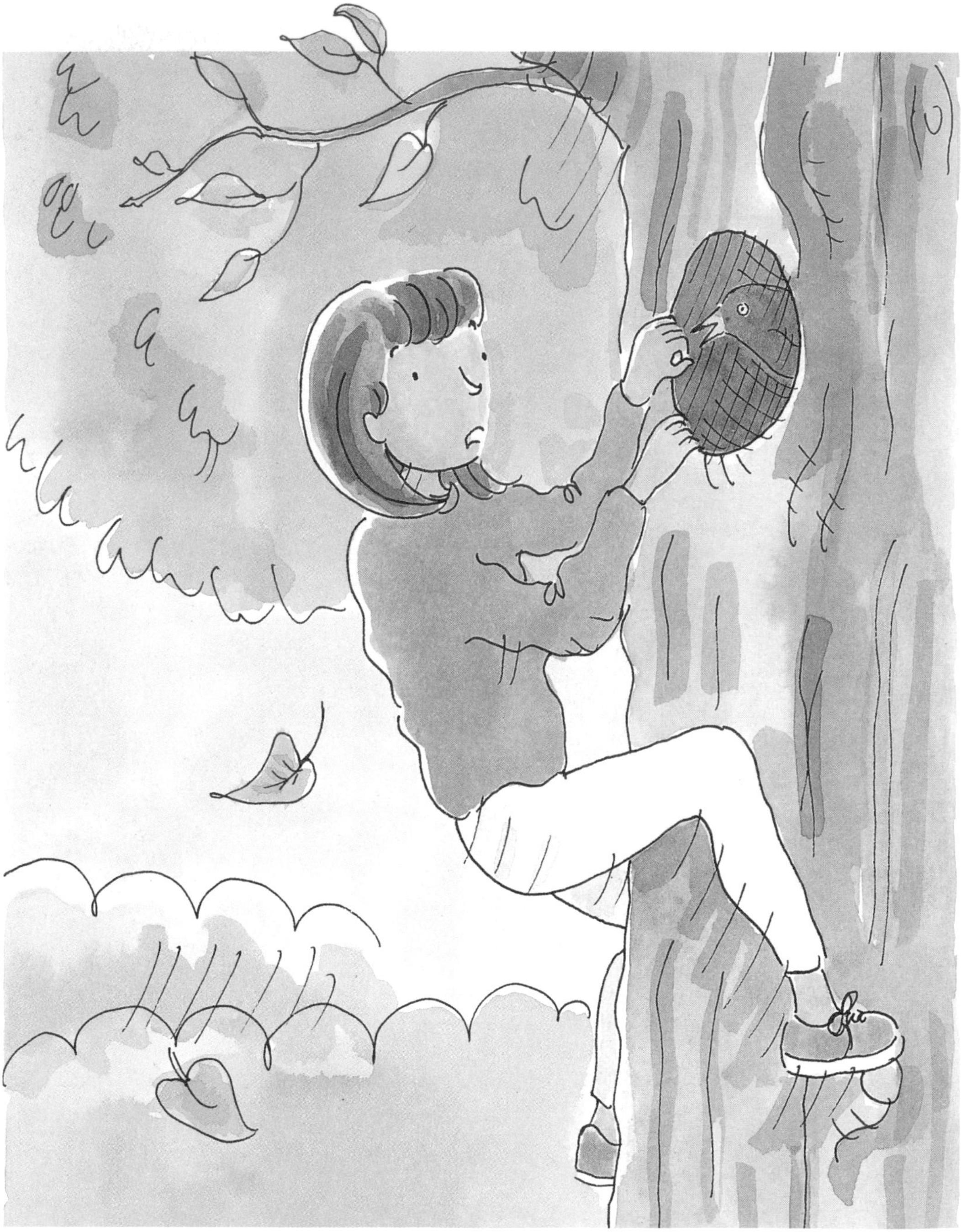

No.

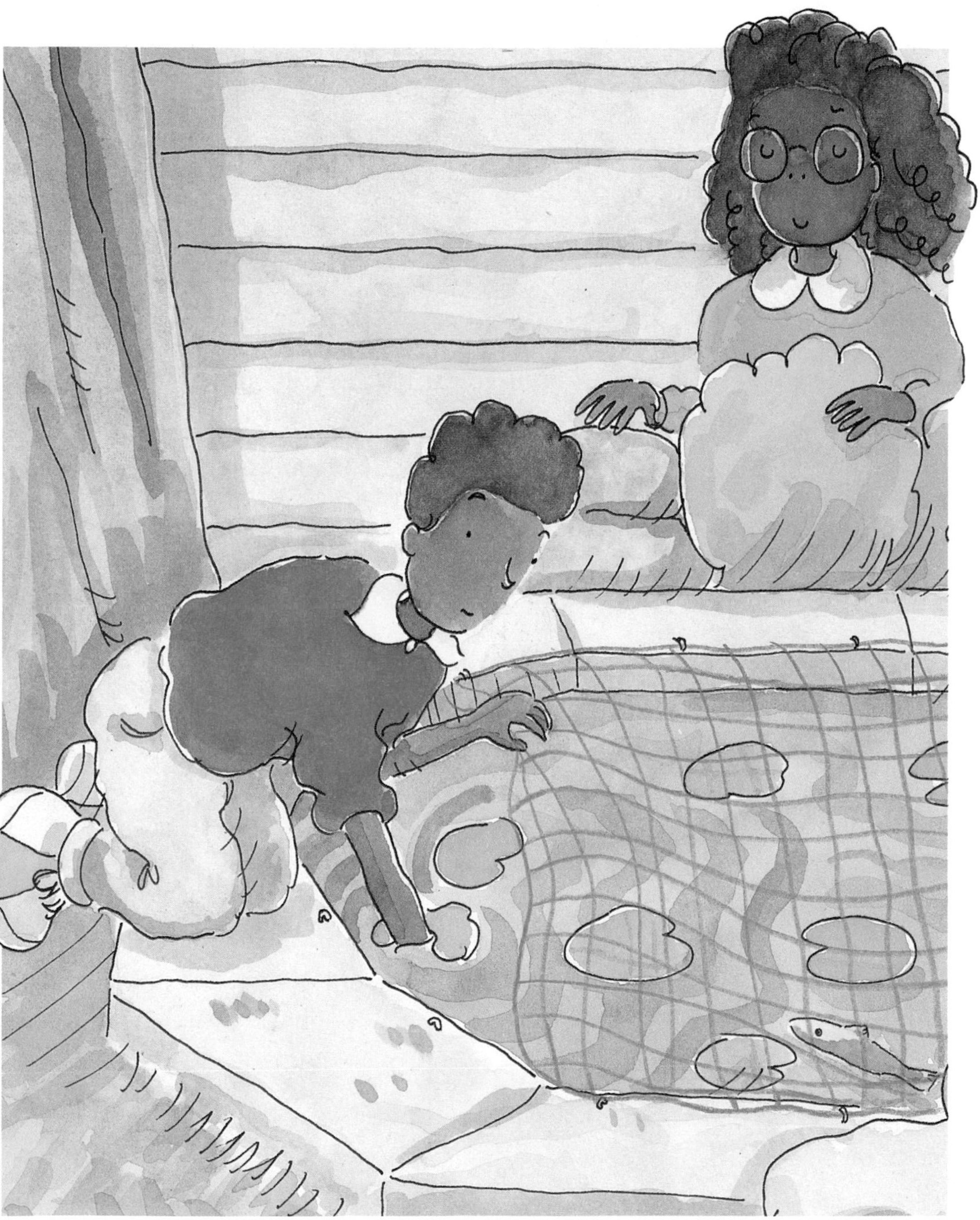

Look in here.

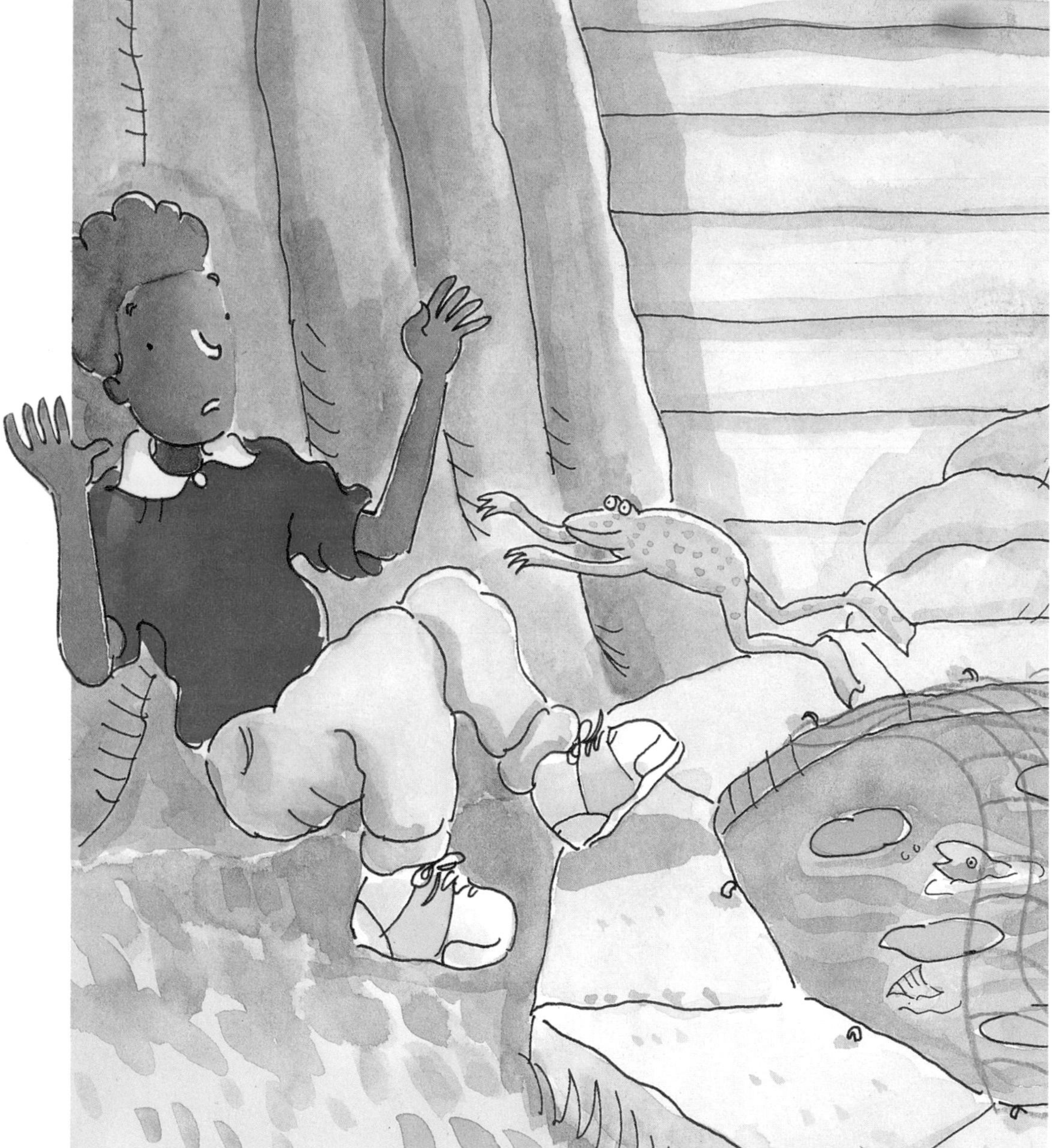

Not in here.

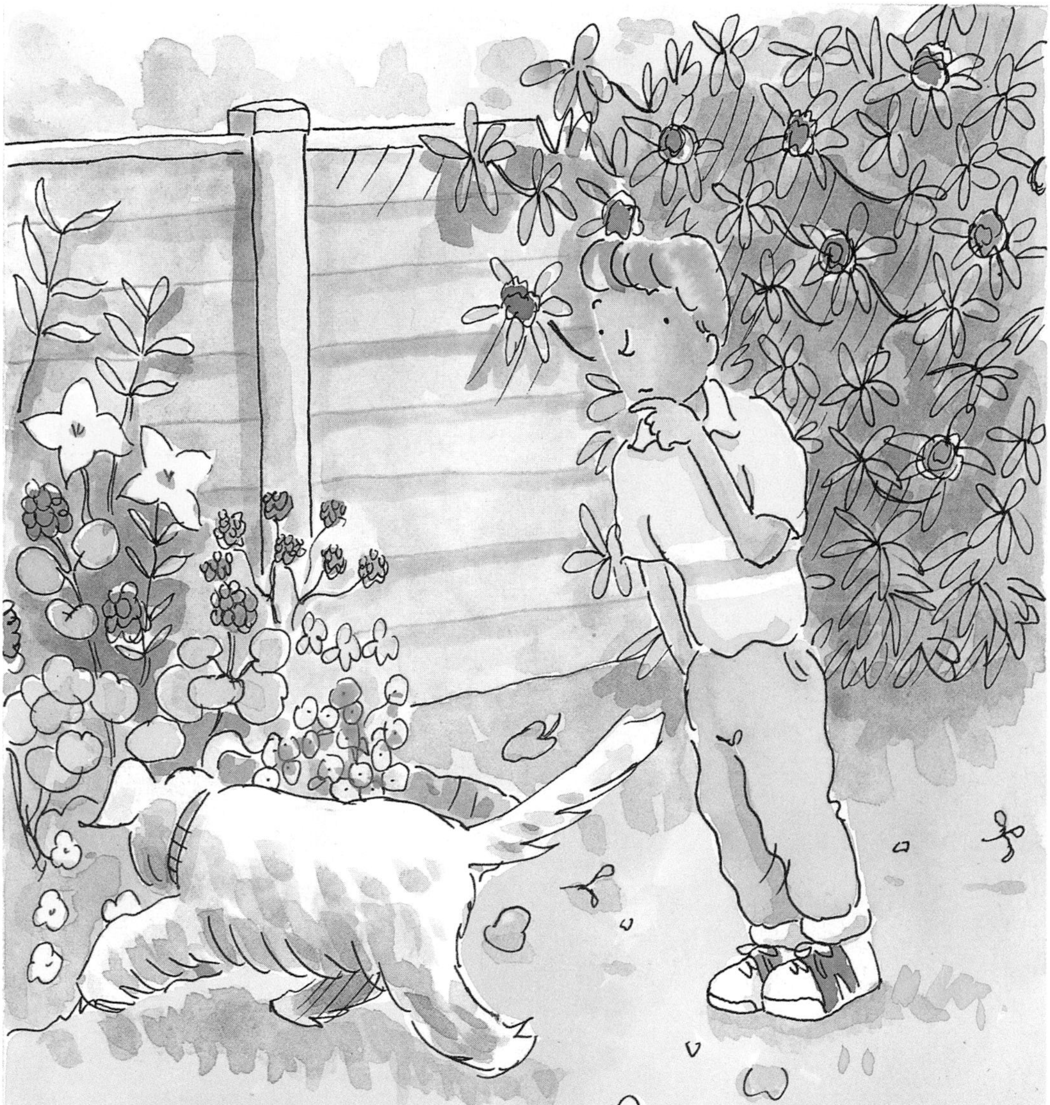

Look in here.

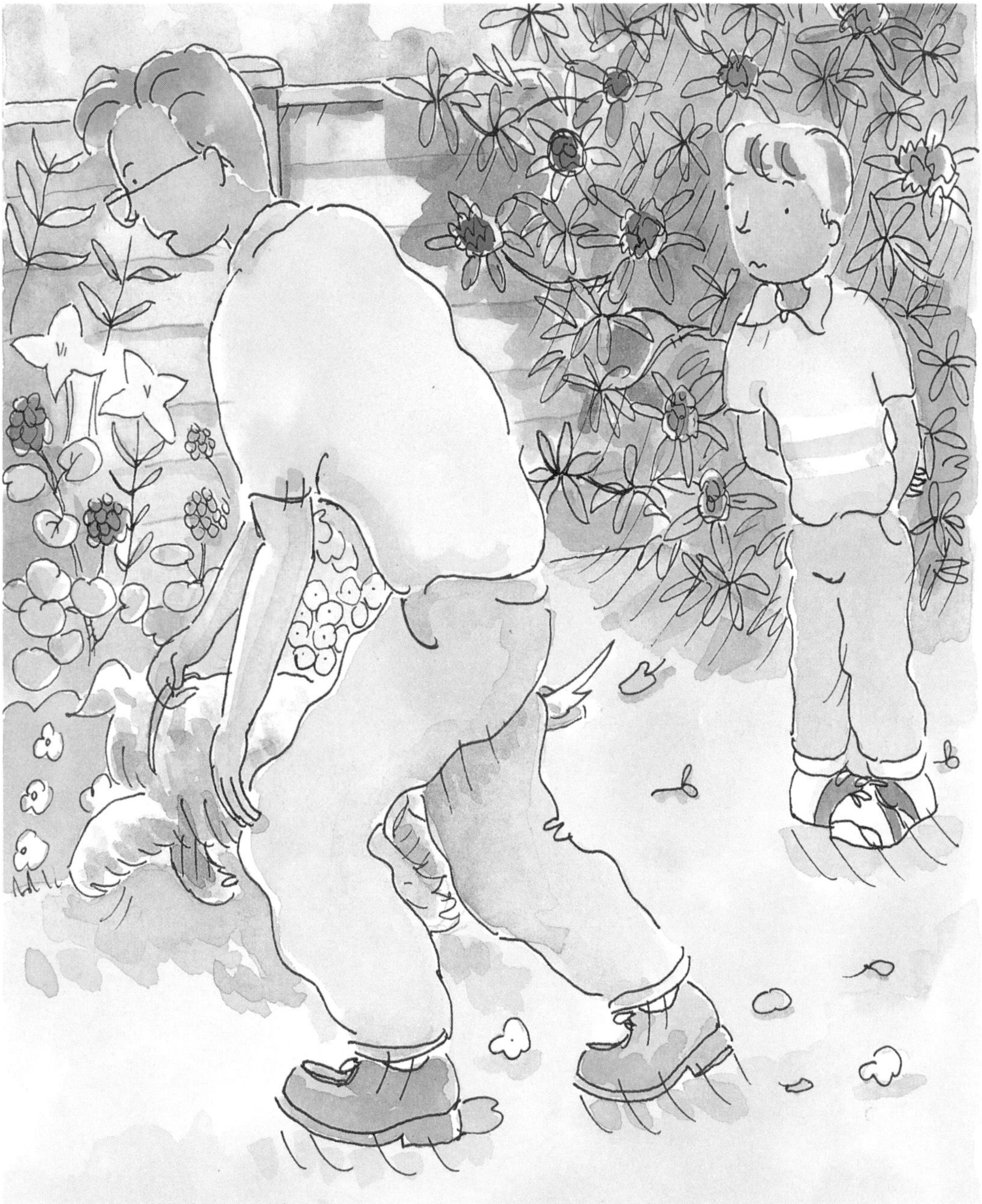

Not in here.

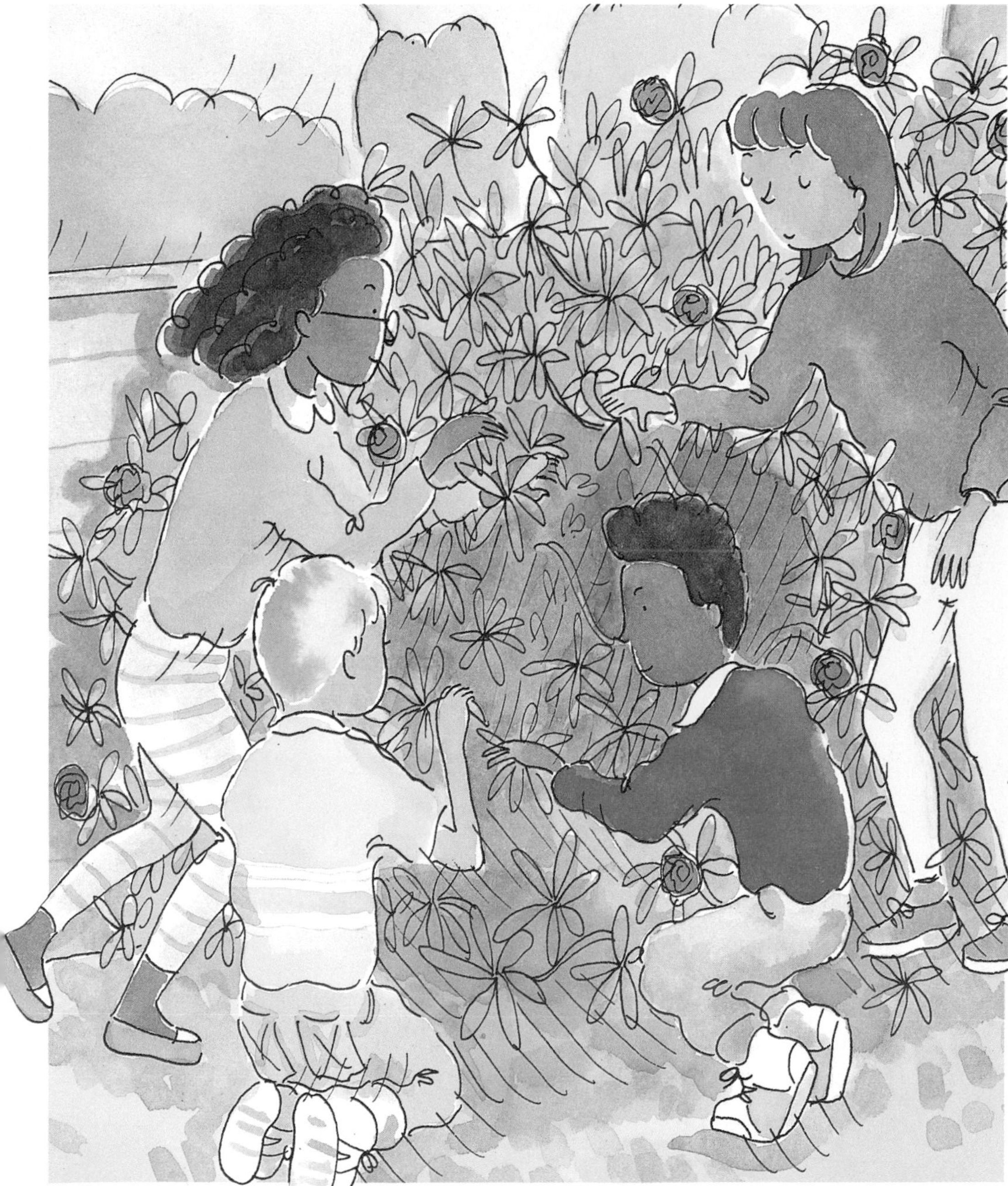

Look in here.

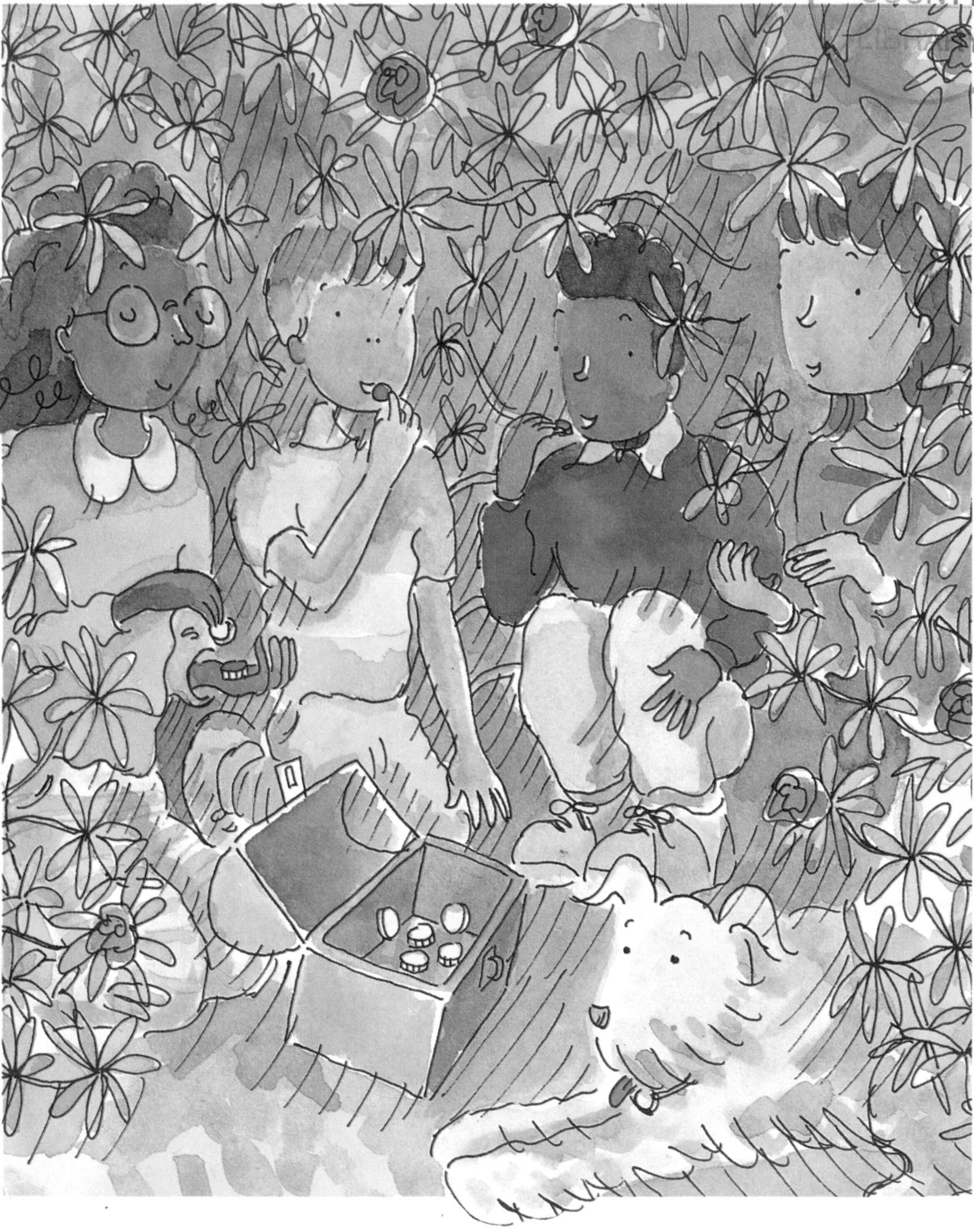

Yes, in here.